Meet My School Counselor; Mrs. Sparks

Written by:
Rebecca Groves Brannock, Ph.D.

Illustrated by:
Janice Hawkins

1

Meet My School Counselor; Mrs. Sparks
Written by: Rebecca Groves Brannock, Ph.D.
& Illustrated by: Janice Hawkins
©2020
JETT Publishing

ISBN: 978-1-7352265-0-7

This book is dedicated to my mentor, H. Rozanne Sparks, on left.
Thanks for teaching me what a great school counselor should be!
I learned from the best.

Allow me to introduce myself! My name is Helen Jane and I am in the third grade. I now live at home with my Dad and younger brother and my little dog named Lily.

When I was halfway in the 1st grade, my whole family moved and I had to start going to a new school. Mrs. Sparks, who was the school counselor at Murphy Elementary, greeted me on the first day. She made me feel so welcome by showing me all around the school and introducing me to a "new buddy" at lunch, Becky Sue.

I love to learn, especially reading and spelling, which are my favorite subjects in school. I also really liked it when my school counselor came into my classes at my old school to teach us lessons about kindness and being a good friend and what to do if someone tries to bully you. Mrs. Sparks said she would do that too, which made me happy.

Mrs. Sparks even had me join a small group with other new students. I enjoyed that a lot, even though I was afraid to go at first. It really helped me not miss my old friends so much. I started to feel like I belonged at my new school. I heard she even did "lunch bunch" groups with students, who met with Mrs. Sparks to work on things they wanted to do better.

Something else I liked about my new school was something called a "Buddy Bench" that was on the playground. It was an idea my school counselor had so everyone would have someone to play with at recess. I thought that was a super idea!

One of the students in my class, Glenn, got brain cancer. Mrs. Sparks asked each of the classrooms to save as many pennies as possible to donate to cancer research. She called it "Pennies for Cancer." My class even won the prize for bringing in the most pennies. How cool was that? It made us all feel good to know we were helping Glenn.

The end of that school year was sad to have to say goodbye to my new friends, but Mrs. Sparks was there to wave good-bye to us after our end-of-the-year picnic, where we played lots of relay games outside, ate hotdogs, and even made s'mores. Yum! That was so much fun!

Then after that summer when I started the 2nd grade, my Mom got really sick. She was diagnosed with cancer and she died. I was so sad all of the time and could not tell anyone how I felt. My Dad was sad too, and so was my little brother. I did not feel like I had anyone to talk to about it. My school counselor listened and she let me cry when I started to think about my Mom not being around anymore. She even gave me a stuffed bunny that was named HOPE. Hope brought me a lot of comfort when I was missing my Mom. That helped me a lot. Mrs. Sparks was there when I needed her most.

When 3rd grade began, I was in a new classroom with several students I did not know. Some of them made fun of me because I didn't have a Mom and because I looked different from them, since I was from the Philippine Islands. Mrs. Sparks came into our classroom to teach us about not making fun of others just because someone was different. That helped so much! After that, I started to feel hope again.

Later this year I met some kids in my class who said they did not have enough food to eat at home. I told my teacher and she let the school counselor know. That made me sad to think I had enough food to eat and they didn't. I wanted to get them some help. Mrs. Sparks was so awesome to help by sending food backpacks home on the weekends for them.

Next year in 4th grade, Mrs. Sparks said she would help us at the end of the year, to get ready for middle school. That is going to be scary for so many kids since we heard that in middle school we have to change classrooms. We also know we are going to have combination locks on our lockers. Other 4th graders said the school counselor helped them by doing a lesson that let them practice opening locks. That made us feel much better!

When I get to high school, I heard that there is more than one school counselor there. They will help me decide where to go to college, so I can become a school counselor just like Mrs. Sparks. I want to be able to help kids the way she always helped me. I think that would be the best career!

Thanks Mrs. Sparks, for being my hero and for showing how much you care for me and other kids too. By the way, I still have my bunny, Hope, that you gave me after my Mom died. Thanks to you, I was able to add more hope back into my life a number of times. You helped a lot!

To learn more about how school counselors can help students be successful, go to www.schoolcounselor.org

School Counselors Make a World of Difference with Their Students!

Meet the writer:

Rebecca Groves Brannock, on right, has been an educator
spanning a career of four decades. She has experience working as a
vocational home economics teacher, a school counselor, and for the past
25 years has been a counselor educator at Pittsburg State University in
Kansas. She and her husband, Jim, of nearly 37 years, reside in Webb
City, MO, with their dog, Miss Elli, and cat, Frankie Mae. Daughter,
Lana, lives in GA with her husband and four grands. When she is not
teaching, "Becky" likes to garden, can her produce, continues writing for
publication, and stays active with her church family.

Meet the illustrator:

Janice Hawkins is an artist, interior designer and event planner. She has painted murals and designed interiors for over 20 years in several states. She teaches painting and creativity classes to all ages. She oversees the prophetic art at Dayspring Church in Springfield Mo. Her passion is nurturing the creatives, helping them dream and discover their creative identity. Janice and Becky met in college, they were college roommates many years ago. From the very first day they met their friendship was formed into a lasting bond, that heart connection has remained strong through the years. Janice currently lives in Republic Mo but teaches and creates wherever she is invited. She has been married to Wayne for 42 years. They have 3 grown children, 2 sons and a daughter that have blessed them with 8 very fun grandchildren! Janice is always on a creative adventure somewhere whether it is in her studio or out on location, you can follow her on Facebook @JaniceHawkinsArt and on Instagram @janicehawkinsart

Questions for Discussion:

1. What is one way a school counselor could help you or your friends?

2. Have you ever had someone you were close to die?

3. Have you or someone you know been made fun of because of being different from others?

4. What is something your elementary school counselor could do to help students in need?

5. Was there anything else you learned from this story about Helen and how she was helped by Mrs. Sparks?

6. Is there a project your school could do to help others in need?

Classroom Activity Ideas

Diversity:

• Play music from one of the countries being taught in geography class. Ask students what they think of the music and how it makes them feel? They could draw a picture of those feelings, with pictures being displayed on the classroom bulletin board along with facts and pictures of the country.

• Teach children how to say hello and goodbye in the first language of EL students in their grade or classroom.

• Have students bring a cookie recipe from their family's culture. Let the class vote on their favorite one. The teacher or school counselor could bake it outside of class, then bring it to share with the class for the next lesson on how family traditions can be an important part of one's culture.

Kindness:

• For large group discussion, ask students to share when they have seen others showing kindness and how the kindness was shown.

• Have students pair up with a partner and brainstorm ways that kindness could be demonstrated at their school. Students can share their ideas with the rest of the class. Have them vote on the top three and present their ideas to the school counselor or principal.

• During National Random Acts of Kindness Week, have students write ways they have demonstrated kindness to others on a strip of paper or how someone demonstrated kindness to them. Collect the strips of paper in each class, staple the strips together to make a chain and display them in the hallway or commons area as a visual of how much kindness is shown at their school.

• Read Have you filled your bucket today? (appropriate for grades K-5). Have students write down on a slip of paper with their name, how they have filled others' buckets within a week time period during National Random Acts of Kindness Week. Do this in each class. The students who have the most slips by the end of the week will be recognized at an assembly or by intercom announcement.

Loss:

- Using incomplete sentences with students in individual or group sessions could be helpful. Some examples are: The thing that makes me feel the saddest is…One thing I liked to do with the person who died was…. After the death, school…. If I could talk to the person who died I would ask….

- Fold a piece of paper in half. On one side have the child draw a picture of his or her family before the death. On the other side, have the child draw a picture of the family after the death. Have the child share the picture with someone who they feel cares and explain the picture.

New Students:

- Pair a new student with a current student when they enroll in your school and have that student accompany the new student to lunch, recess, the playground, etc.

- Have new students complete an "All About Me" mini poster when they enroll. This can be displayed on a new student bulletin board in the hallway or within individual classrooms.

School Counselors:

- During National School Counseling Week, the first full week of February, have students create posters to display around the school of how school counselors help students. The best posters could be used in the future on the school counselor's website. They could also be downsized and printed into notecards to use as thank you's to send to the school counseling advisory council members for serving on the committee.

Transitions:

- Have students create a skit to welcome new students to their school, which could be used at a new student reception at the beginning of each school year.

Additional Resources for School Counselors, Teachers and Parents:

Diversity:
- Child fun multicultural activities: tinyurl.com/ycutpp4
- Diverse family toolkit: www.pacer.org (free videos and guides)
- Race bridges for schools: racebridgesstudio.com
- Teachers First multicultural resources: teachersfirst.com/multicult.htm
- Teaching Tolerance magazine: www.teachingtolerance.org (free subscription for educators)

Kindness:
- Random Acts of Kindness Week: www.randomactsofkindness.org
- Kindness cards available on Teachers Pay Teachers site: www.teacherspayteachers.com/prodiuct/pass-kindness-forward-card-3635576
- Dneirf by Mike Resh: Appropriate for K-6. Free downloadable handouts and lessons plans accompany the book at www.mikeresh.com
- Start now you can make a difference by Chelsea Clinton: Appropriate for ages 6-9.

Loss:
- Coalition for supporting grieving students: https://grievingstudents.org
- Peter's Place: www.petersplaceonline.org
- The Dougy Center: www.dougy.org

New Students:
- Teacher vision website for K-12 resources: Teachervision.com/teaching-strategies/getting-know-your-students

School Counselors:
- The essential role of elementary school counselors brief (updated in 2019): schoolcounselor.org/asca/media/asca/Careers-Roles/WhyElem.pdf

Transitions:
- Resources for teachers: Edutopia.org/blog/transition-resources-teachers-matt-davis
- Parent tool kit: parenttoolkit.com/academics/news/back-to-school/guiding-our-children-through-school-transitions-elementary-school

Other books by this author:

The many faces of Helen Jane

A story about diversity, acceptance, empathy and kindness